THE DOJO

SIDE CONTROL

BY PATRICK JONES

darbycreek
MINNEAPOLIS

Darby Creek
A division of Lerner Publishing Group, Inc.
241 First Avenue North
Minneapolis, MN 55401 U.S.A.

Website address: www.lernerbooks.com

The images in this book are used with the permission of: © iStockphoto.com/
Stephen Morris (fighters); © iStockphoto.com/Tim Messick (background);
© iStockphoto.com/Erkki Makkonen (metal wires); © iStockphoto.com/
TommL (punching fist), © iStockphoto.com/dem10 (barbed wire).

Main body text set in Janson Text LT Std 12/17.5.
Typeface provided by Linotype AG.

Library of Congress Cataloging-in-Publication Data

Jones, Patrick, 1961–
    Side control / by Patrick Jones.
        pages   cm. — (The dojo ; #2)
    ISBN 978–1–4677–0631–5 (lib. bdg. : alk. paper)
    ISBN 978–1–4677–1632–1 (eBook)
    [1. Mixed martial arts—Fiction. 2. Military service, Voluntary—Fiction.
3. African Americans—Fiction.] I. Title.
PZ7.J7242Si 2013
[Fic]—dc23   2012042250

Manufactured in the United States of America
1 – SB – 7/15/13

IN MEMORY OF
MILES KLEIN
-P.J.

WELCOME TO

If you're already a fan of mixed martial arts, in particular the Ultimate Fighting Championship (UFC), then you're probably familiar with moves like triangle choke, spinning heel kick, and Kimura. If not, check out the MMA terms and weight classes in the back of the book. You can also go online for videos of famous fights and training videos. Amateur fights are similar to the pros but require more protection for the fighters. While there are unified rules, each state allows for variation.

WELCOME TO THE DOJO.

STEP INSIDE.

CHAPTER 1

"I'm sorry, Jackson, but I don't think you're ready," the new army recruiter says.

Jackson James sinks into the hard chair as the recruiter stares at the computer screen.

"I'm not seeing what Corporal Davis saw." Corporal Richards turns to Jackson, forehead scrunched. "Now, we're not just talking about joining the army. Do you really think you have what it takes to apply for Special Forces duty?"

"Yes, sir!" Jackson controls his urge to salute the crew-cut-wearing white officer.

"Being in the Army Special Forces is part

of being a team, but I see you played no team sports other than football, your freshman year, and you even quit that."

"I'm training in mixed martial arts." Jackson's voice fills with pride. "Corporal Davis said it was the hardest physical training available and would best prepare me for Special Forces."

"Maybe physical training, but the Special Forces are a team, understand?"

Jackson balls his fist. He doesn't appreciate being talked to like a little boy when he's turning eighteen in a few months.

"Let me ask, Jackson, why did you quit football your freshman year?"

Jackson pauses. It's a trick question. If he's looked at Jackson's file, then he knows the answer. He's testing Jackson's honesty and integrity. "I didn't quit. I got kicked off the team."

The recruiter hesitates for a moment. "We don't need discipline problems in Special Forces."

"I wasn't a discipline problem. I obeyed my coaches. But I got . . . arrested."

"You have a juvenile record?" The recruiter

raises an eyebrow. Jackson knows that look. It means the recruiter no longer sees a potential soldier but just another black kid from the hood—even though Jackson lives in the St. Louis burbs. His mom, a lawyer, is probably better educated than the recruiter. But that makes no difference.

Jackson exhales. "I was arrested, detained, and then released," he says. "I tried to get back on the football team, but Coach Cole said he didn't give second chances."

No response from the corporal.

"It was a mistake." Jackson wipes sweat from his brow, even though it's a bitterly cold January day. "I was making bad choices and hanging with the wrong crowd."

"Remember, son, you're only as good as the company you keep."

Jackson nods his head in agreement, thinking back to bad memories of before he joined the Missouri MMA dojo. He lacked purpose and self-confidence. "I know that now."

"We like to see proof that recruits have the dedication to work together and work hard and the discipline to balance that with their school-work. Without any kind of team sports, I don't see how you're preparing yourself for this kind of challenge."

"The dojo takes teamwork, sir. And trust," Jackson replies, looking Corporal Richards in the eye. "Plus I'm doing better at school, and I'm working in MMA around that." Jackson rubs his sore right shoulder. His judo instructor, Mr. Matsuda, almost tore if off demonstrating the Americana submission yesterday in his MMA class. *Come to the dojo,* Jackson thinks—*I'll show you a challenge.* "I can pass the ASVAB." Jackson sits up, chin thrust forward. He's passed the practice military entrance exam many times, although he still struggles with the math section.

"And what about the physical exam? Are you prepared for that?"

Jackson leaps from the chair, takes off his green army jacket and his white T-shirt, and then sprawls onto the ugly brown carpet. "Fifty push-ups in two minutes. Time me."

Corporal Richards laughs. "Jackson, you don't need to do that."

"Time me!"

"Fine, suit yourself." Richards looks at his watch and then yells, "Go!"

By the time Richards yells stop, Jackson's at fifty-four. "Now, sit-ups," Jackson says.

Jackson clears sixty sit-ups a few seconds before time is up. Richards applauds, looking surprised. "That's quite a performance. Now, use your last semester to show you can really dedicate yourself to school as well as your training, and stay away from bad influences, and then I'd probably recommend you for Special Forces."

"Thanks." Jackson puts his T-shirt and jacket back on and returns to the chair.

"It says here you first visited this office three years ago, so you must be ready to go."

Jackson looks at the floor. "I am, but I might not sign up on my eighteenth birthday like I said."

Richards leans across the desk. "Huh. I thought you were committed. What is it, a girl?"

"I wish," Jackson mumbles. The girls in his MMA dojo are off-limits, and girls at school go for guys with more money.

"Then what's the problem?" Corporal Richards presses.

"I am committed, but I like MMA too," Jackson says. "I went to the dojo at first just for the training, but I like MMA and I'm good at it. Once I'm eighteen, I want to fight amateur status, and then maybe see if I can go pro. If not, then I'll join right away. One way or another, Jackson James will be a Green Beret."

"It helps that your father served his country. Special Forces, too—that's a plus."

Jackson looks at the posters on the wall with the words *duty*, *honor*, and *sacrifice*. The words pound Jackson like hammer fists from the mount. He takes a deep breath. "Sir, my father didn't just serve his country. He died for it."

CHAPTER 2

"Ready?" Mr. Hodge asks Jackson. Jackson nods. Mr. Hodge asks the same question of Hector Morales, who stands across the ring from Jackson. Hector nods and bangs his gloves against his face. Jackson readjusts his sparring helmet and waits for the whistle.

Mr. Hodge blows the whistle, and Jackson rushes toward the center of the ring. He and Hector have sparred and trained together for two years. Along with Nong and Meghan, they're the only ones left from Mr. Hodge's first teen MMA program. In five months, they'll all graduate from high school, but before that, they'll turn eighteen and step into the cage for their first amateur fights.

Jackson circles Hector, looking to shoot, but Hector defends with offensive strikes. An overhand left doesn't connect, nor does a right uppercut, but Hector lands a solid roundhouse kick in Jackson's side. Jackson pounds his gloves together, angry at himself for taking the kick.

Of course Hector—a middleweight, two weight classes under Jackson—would be using his speed, Jackson thinks. He calls Hector a drive-by fighter because Hector does his damage and then gets away.

"Work, Hector, work!" Mr. Hodge yells out from Hector's corner.

"Be aggressive, not angry. Control your emotions!" Mr. Matsuda shouts from Jackson's corner. Jackson listens and then breathes to let his frustration go. When he entered the dojo at fifteen, he didn't know how to fight. By obeying his coach's orders, he's grown into a skilled MMA warrior.

Hector lands a hard left hook and goes into

the clinch. He wraps his hands around the back of Jackson's neck and brings up his right knee. Jackson eats it but drops down, grabs Hector's vulnerable left leg, and drives him hard to the mat. Both are fighting for position, but Jackson lands on top and fights his way to side control.

Jackson stretches his legs out behind him, driving Hector onto his back. With his left arm, Jackson tries to control Hector's neck. He uses his right to throw short punches from the top.

"Move, Hector, move!" Mr. Hodge yells.

"Americana!" Mr. Matsuda yells, as if he's reading Jackson's mind. Jackson grabs Hector's left wrist with his left arm. Then he wedges his elbow down the side of Hector's head and pins Hector's left arm down like a pretzel. Hector tries to straighten his arm out, but Jackson's grip is tight. Even as Hector fights to regain control of his left, Jackson weaves his right hand under Hector's left arm. Jackson brings his hands together and starts to crank when the whistle blows.

Jackson releases the hold and stands. He extends his hand to Hector and helps him to the mat. They touch gloves, then hug. "You've been working on submissions?" Hector asks.

Jackson nods as Hector returns to his corner to confer with Mr. Hodge.

"Great execution!" Mr. Matsuda pats Jackson on the back. "Side control is the key. Everybody wants a full mount, but that limits you. Side control gives your opponent nothing and leaves you with many options. It doesn't win the fight, but it creates opportunities. Choose the right one and you win!"

c c c c c

"Can I talk to you, Mr. Hodge?" Jackson asks. The dojo master nods and hands Jackson a jump rope, and they jump together.

"My last semester of school is going to be tough," Jackson says, sounding unsure.

"I see."

"The army recruiter says I've got to focus on my schoolwork even more."

Hodge picks up the pace of his jumping. The sweat starts to break along his scarred forehead. "Are you saying you need to quit?"

"I might just have to miss some nights," Jackson mumbles.

"No, I need committed athletes. You're so close to reaching your goal."

"I'm still committed," Jackson says. "But the army recruiter said—,"

"You do what you think is best," Mr. Hodge says almost in a fatherly tone. *The problem,* Jackson thinks, *is I don't know what that is.* He just knows what he wants to be: a Special Forces soldier like his father . . . and an MMA champion like Mr. Hodge.

Jackson throws down the jump rope and throws punches against the speed bag. The smack of his hands thunders over the other noise in the dojo. He doesn't want to go against Mr. Hodge, but he doesn't want to disregard Corporal Richards's advice either. "How about if I also train on Saturdays with the adults?"

"That's against my rules. You're still a teenager and—,"

"I'll almost eighteen," Jackson says. "Besides, I need the challenge, better competition." He punches the bag harder a few times to make his point and then turns to Mr. Hodge.

Mr. Hodge, still bouncing, stares at Jackson's pleading eyes. Finally, he sighs. "Okay, we can try it."

"Thanks," Jackson says, relieved he didn't need to beg.

"Jackson, you won't be thanking me after the first time a grown man puts you to sleep."

Jackson kisses his right glove, curls his face into his best scowl, and throws a vicious hook. "Ain't no man gonna stop Jackson James from getting what he wants."

Mr. Hodge stops jumping. "Only one person can beat you, Jackson. That person is you."

CHAPTER 3

"Jackson! Joseph! The James gang! What's going on?" Hakeem offers his fist to Jackson and his little brother, Joseph. Jackson ignores it, but Joseph returns the gesture.

"Nothing. Just busy." Jackson walks a little quicker, but Joseph slows down.

Hakeem follows Jackson and Joseph into the corner store. Once inside, Hakeem shadows Jackson, staying just behind. When they played football freshman year, Hakeem was quarterback, while Jackson snapped the ball. Hakeem still calls the plays on their block, but like Jackson, he hasn't touched a football in years.

"Hurry up!" Jackson yells at Joseph and walks away from Hakeem.

Hakeem walks over to the magazine rack. He picks up a copy of *Flex* featuring a UFC fighter on the cover and shows it to Jackson, smirking. "Hey, look, is this you?"

"It's Jon Jones," Jackson says. He's proud to share his initials with his idol.

"I bet to the people who put this magazine out, all brothers look alike," Hakeem says.

"Looks more like me," Joseph says. Three years apart, Jackson and Joseph could have once passed for twins, but years of MMA training have turned Jackson's baby fat into solid muscle.

"So you're like, all ultimate fighter, right? You think that makes you some kind of tough guy?" Hakeem asks. Jackson grunts a non-response and picks up some milk and soup for his mom. The prices at the corner store are high, but she hasn't had time to get to a supermarket.

"What's with you?" Hakeem grabs Jackson's right arm. Jackson stares him down.

"You used to be fun. Now look at you, all serious," Hakeem says and laughs. Jackson doesn't join in. Hakeem finally walks away as Jackson grabs a few more cans off the shelves. He takes everything to the counter and hands over a twenty. The counter guy takes the money but never takes his eyes off Jackson. When Jackson opens the door to leave, Hakeem cuts in front of him. Joseph follows quickly behind Jackson. Jackson senses the counter guy is still watching him.

"That place is a rip-off," Jackson mutters as they walk across the store's parking lot.

"I know, so I returned the favor." Hakeem unzips his black hoodie. Inside are three candy bars. He hands one each to Jackson and Joseph. "Like I said, just like old times."

Jackson's hungry—he's always hungry—but he waves it off. Hakeem rips the wrapper off his candy bar, tosses it onto the snowy sidewalk, and devours the candy in four bites.

Jackson hits Hakeem with another hard stare before he bends over to pick up the candy wrapper.

"I'll take his," Joseph says. Hakeem hands the third candy bar to Joseph. Jackson frowns.

"We're mobbing that store tomorrow night, if you want in," Hakeem says.

Jackson walks faster with his head down. "Listen, Hakeem, leave us alone."

Hakeem grabs Jackson's arm and squeezes. "Or else? What you gonna do about it?"

Jackson gives his fiercest scowl and lifts Hakeem's hand off his arm. "Whatever I want."

"I don't know," Hakeem says as a smirk spreads across his face. "Seems like all you want is to be a good little soldier."

Joseph laughs but stifles it quickly.

Jackson stares at Hakeem and then at Joseph. "Joseph, let's go!" Jackson's voice booms as he starts jogging toward home. When he doesn't hear Joseph behind him, he turns and sees Hakeem walking the other way, with Joseph following one step behind.

Jackson thinks of chasing after Joseph, but he walks home instead. He could warn Joseph about Hakeem, but it wouldn't do any good. *The only way a person learns anything,* Jackson thinks—*in the cage or outside of it—is by making painful mistakes.*

CHAPTER 4

"Look at the new fish," Nong says quietly to Jackson and laughs too loud. They're doing pull-ups before practice. Hector jumps rope nearby, while Meghan smashes her fists into the heavy punching bag, hitting harder and talking less than anyone except Jackson. As usual.

Jackson glances at Mr. Hodge talking to four new students. The latest generation. Jackson couldn't even have gotten into the dojo's teen program with Mr. Hodge's current rules requiring new students to have experience in one MMA field. All Jackson had when he started was strength and an eye toward making Special Forces.

"Hey, Meghan, you got some competition!" Nong says and points toward the tall, blonde girl and a shorter black girl. "Maybe one of you can finally get a girlfriend."

"You know Mr. Hodge doesn't allow that," Hector says. Jackson mumbles in agreement as he stares at the shorter girl. He's seen her around North High. Tyresha Harris, a senior.

"I'm hitting the dummy." Jackson adjusts his gloves, then walks over and picks up one of the heavy wrestling dummies. He hurls it to the mat in a textbook back throw and starts punching. In the black dummy canvas, he sees Hakeem's face. Right, left, right.

"Jackson, let's use that energy elsewhere!" Mr. Hodge shouts and waves Jackson over.

Jackson nods. He throws one last punch, which almost dents the bag with his WMD-force right. Jackson laughs as he walks over to Mr. Hodge, remembering what the great Pride fighter Cro Cop said about the effects of his head kicks on an opponent: "Right leg, hospital—left leg, cemetery." It's similar to how Jackson describes his punches.

"Jackson, this is Nong's cousin Lue Vang. Also, Rex Taylor, Tyresha Harris, and Heather Brock, our new recruits," Mr. Hodge says. "Lue and Heather have black belts in karate. Rex is a Golden Gloves champ. Tyresha was a champion wrestler at North High. Best group since yours."

Jackson nods at the new students and then keeps his eyes down. Both guys look smaller than heavyweight, so while Hector and Nong get fresh meat, Jackson gets no new challenge. Except to try not to stare at Tyresha.

"Rex, get ready and then get in the ring," Mr. Hodge says. Rex does as he's told. They all do as they're told. Jackson wishes he would've thought to tell the recruiter, *I'm good at taking orders.*

Jackson puts on his boxing gear and steps into the ring. He's bouncing on his heels, throwing punches, and visualizing the spar. If the kid's a Golden Gloves champion, he probably can move. *He can run,* Jackson thinks, *but he can't hide.* For as hard a punch as Jackson throws, there's one thing harder: his chin. He'll patiently take ten strikes on the chin to get in one when the fighter makes a mistake. Ten punches that connect score points, but one shot that bangs ends a fight. Good night.

"Jackson, come here," Mr. Matsuda says as he waves Jackson to the corner. "Let's teach these newbies some respect right away."

Jackson nods. Mr. Hodge is the dojo master, but Mr. Matsuda's acted as Jackson's main teacher. He's molded him from a brawler into a grappler with both knockout power and submission savvy.

"Let's do three two-minute rounds. Just boxing, okay?" Mr. Hodge says. Jackson and Rex touch gloves in the center of the ring. When Mr. Hodge blows the whistle, Rex sticks and moves as Jackson suspected, throwing a quick jab and then backing away while Jackson speeds ahead. Rex connects, but to Jackson, it feels like Rex is swatting flies. As Rex jabs, Jackson's mind wanders to the recruiter, to Hakeem, to his mom, and to Joseph. A left hook to the body returns

Jackson's focus. *Poor Rex just poked an angry lion with a stick*, Jackson thinks.

When Rex tries another hook to the body, he leaves his chin open. A hard right and Rex hits the mat. Mr. Hodge and Mr. Matsuda run into the ring. Mr. Hodge looks concerned at the dazed glare in Rex's eyes. Jackson kisses his right fist as he watches Mr. Matsuda beam with pride.

⬚ ⬚ ⬚ ⬚ ⬚ ⬚

"You know *welcome mat* doesn't mean you welcome a new fighter by putting them on the mat," Nong says. Meghan and Hector laugh, but Jackson just pulls his oversized army jacket around him. They're outside the dojo, letting the cold breeze refresh them.

Jackson shrugs. "I told him I was sorry."

"He thought it was Hector talking in Spanish after you scrambled his brain," Nong says.

"Maybe you don't have new competition, but I do," Meghan says before downing an energy drink. "Tyresha is fierce. And for a cheerleader type, that girl Heather throws mean kicks."

"She's got to change her name," Nong says. "Who is going to be afraid of a Heather?"

"I don't know, Nong, it doesn't sound much worse than calling yourself Ninja Warrior," Meghan says with a laugh.

Jackson's phone buzzes. It's a text from Hakeem. All it has is an address and a time. Jackson turns off the phone.

"You want to get something to eat later?" Nong asks.

"Guys, one second," Jackson says, suddenly quieter.

Meghan rolls her eyes. "And ladies?"

Jackson nods.

"I wanted to tell you that I won't be around as much," Jackson almost whispers. "I have to step it up at school, show the army recruiter I can work hard, and I think it's going to take more time." Nong is nodding. "So I'll train mainly on Saturdays with the adults. Can any of you join me?" Jackson doesn't look any of them in the eye to let them see he's afraid to go it alone.

"I work Saturdays," Hector reminds Jackson.

"And I have to study," Nong says.

"I'm almost eighteen," Meghan says. "Tyresha's almost eighteen, so maybe her too."

Jackson scowls, because it's what he does. Even if he feels more like smiling at the thought of seeing more of Tyresha.

CHAPTER 5

"She sounds like a bad influence," Jackson's mom says as she passes Jackson the bowl of green beans. Jackson takes a second helping and offers it to Joseph, who declines.

"She made a mistake, that's all," Jackson says. He'd just told his mom and Joseph about Tyresha and why she joined the dojo even though the wrestling season isn't over. After she started at Missouri MMA, he had asked around to get her story.

"Well, you learned from your mistake, so I hope she did too."

Jackson nods in agreement. After he and Hakeem were arrested, he cut Hakeem out of his life. He wonders if Tyresha will make better choices after getting kicked off the wrestling team for failing a drug test. Mr. Hodge doesn't test, but he has zero tolerance. If he even suspects you're using, you're gone. No exceptions.

"Are you feeling okay?" Jackson's mom asks Joseph, who is picking at his food.

"May I be excused?" Joseph answers.

"We're a family, and we eat dinner together," Jackson's mom answers.

Joseph half laughs and grunts, turning away from Jackson's glare. Jackson asks his mom about her latest case with the city. He asks because he's interested, but also so she won't ask him any more questions.

When Jackson finally finishes dinner, his mom nods and Joseph leaves the table.

"He's who you should be worrying about, not me," Jackson says when he hears Joseph's door slam shut. He wants to warn his mom about Hakeem and Joseph, but he knows how disappointed that would make her.

"Joseph's like you were at that age, except you're here to set an example for him."

"And my example was getting arrested."

"Exactly! Joseph knows the consequences of bad choices and what it means to turn your life around."

Jackson says nothing. The best way to avoid bad choices is to avoid thinking of them as choices. It's easier just to obey the rules at home, at school, and in the dojo. Like a good soldier.

᙭ ᙭ ᙭ ᙭ ᙭

Jackson helps his mom do the dishes. She heads to the den to work at her desk, while Jackson sits at the kitchen table. He opens his math book and wonders if the equations would make more sense if he looked at them inside the ring. Jackson thinks about calling Nong for help but decides against it and racks his brain for other people. Hakeem turned most of his old friends against him after freshman year. Jackson glances at a photo on the refrigerator door of his mom and dad, smiling and happy. He pulls out his phone and makes a few calls until he gets the number he wants.

"Hey, Tyresha, it's Jackson James from the dojo," he says when she answers.

There's a pause. He hears Tyresha whisper something and then giggle. "What up?"

"Hey, did you take algebra?" Jackson asks. "I'm lost in this homework."

Another pause. Another whisper. This time more laughter than giggles. "Yeah."

"Do you think you could—," Jackson starts. He hates asking for help.

"I don't know." Tyresha laughs louder. Jackson wonders if she's high. If getting high meant so much to her that she lost her chance to repeat as girls' state wrestling champ, then it might matter more than anything else. Maybe his mom is right about Tyresha. She is about most things.

"So how good is that Meghan chick?" Tyresha asks. "She seems like a bully."

"She's the best of the four of us," Jackson answers. "Nong, Hector, and me all still have holes in our game, but Meghan's a complete fighter. She practically lives at the dojo."

Another pause but no laughter. What is she thinking? In the ring, part of the skill is guessing your opponent's next move. But females leave Jackson confused. "So, math is pretty tough?" she finally offers.

"It's grounding and pounding me," Jackson says. Tyresha laughs a little louder.

"I'll help you with math, if you teach me how to knock people out like you did to Rex."

"Deal," Jackson says. "When do you want to start?"

Jackson pauses as he realizes he's trapped between two bad choices. If he gets into anything with Tyresha, he'll break Mr. Hodge's rules. But turning away from a girl like Tyresha would be stupid—and bad for his math grade. He wonders if some rules are worth breaking. "How about now?"

⬚ ⬚ ⬚ ⬚ ⬚

Jackson knocks on the door of the den to tell his mom he's going out, but she doesn't answer. She's either too busy or too tired from working too hard and has fallen asleep at her desk again. He grabs his army jacket and runs a finger over the stitching with the initials *JJ*. There's not a day that goes by that he doesn't think of his dad, the first Jackson James.

"Joseph, I'm going out," Jackson yells through Joseph's bedroom door, but his brother doesn't answer. Jackson can hear Joseph, Hakeem, and Hakeem's cousin Deshon laughing.

"Joseph, I said I'm going out." Jackson turns the handle, but the door's locked, which isn't allowed. Jackson thinks how Joseph is testing all of his mom's rules, just like he did.

Jackson waits for his chance from his doorway down the hall. When Deshon heads toward the bathroom and leaves Joseph's door open, Jackson slips down the hallway and peeks inside. Joseph and Hakeem are watching TV, eating bags of chips, and passing a fifth of Phillips vodka between them.

Jackson pulls out his phone and looks at Hakeem's last text from yesterday. He knows the address: Al's Corner Store. Most people in the neighborhood know about Al's, but the ones that didn't would have learned about it on last night's news. It was the location of another in a string of flash mob robberies.

CHAPTER 6

"Jackson and Hector, center mat!" Mr. Hodge says.

"Happy Valentine's Day, right?" Hector says before they touch gloves.

Jackson nods. The spars with adults on Saturday shook his confidence, so he's back at teen MMA practice at least for tonight, homework or not. As a bonus, it distracts him from thinking about Joseph robbing stores with Hakeem and Deshon.

Jackson won't turn Hakeem in again, like he did before to cooperate with police. He won't give Hakeem the satisfaction of being right for calling him a snitch. But Jackson wishes he could keep his brother from repeating his own mistakes.

As Jackson and Hector prepare to spar, everybody else keeps drilling except Lue, Heather, and Tyresha, who stand next to Mr. Hodge. Rex isn't there. Nong was right; he was concussed and won't be able to train. Jackson avoids eye contact with Tyresha but keeps her rock-hard abs in his sights.

He and Hector have sparred hundreds of times, and Jackson, with more weight, size, and strength, normally wins. Before the fight starts, Mr. Matsuda comes over to Jackson.

"I want you to make him tap in the first minute," he says. Jackson nods. Mr. Matsuda is always raising the bar. The whistle starts the action, and Hector circles and starts throwing strikes.

"Move, Hector, move!" Mr. Hodge shouts, and Hector responds. He punches, kicks, and throws knees. Jackson's more a human punching bag than a fighter at this point. Jackson tries for the clinch to cut down the distance, but Hector punches out of it. They repeat the dance several times, and each time Hector gets free. Jackson waits for a mistake to pounce.

"One minute left!" Mr. Matsuda shouts, which lights a fire under Jackson. At the next clinch, Hector throws an overhand left that leaves his midsection exposed. Jackson takes the punch so he can capitalize on Hector's mistake. He gut wrenches Hector and throws him to the mat. As they're tumbling down, Jackson gets side control. Once on the mat, he forces Hector onto his back, and his superior strength locks in the rear naked choke in just seconds.

"Hector, tap," Jackson shouts.

"Tap!" Mr. Hodge screams, and Hector taps. Jackson stands and reaches his hand to help Hector. Showing respect for an opponent is a code that Mr. Hodge and Mr. Matsuda demand.

"Good fight," Jackson whispers into Hector's ear as they hug.

"Excellent execution, Jackson!" Mr. Hodge shouts and then bows to Jackson in respect. As

Jackson leaves the ring, Mr. Matsuda gives him a high five.

"Good job, Jon Jones Jr.," Tyresha whispers as Jackson walks past. Jackson covers his face with his glove, pretending to wipe sweat while hiding a smile.

Mr. Hodge calls the students to him. Jackson stands next to Tyresha. She bumps against him as Mr. Hodge starts, "We have four fighters almost ready to enter their first amateur competition. They'll be taking on fighters more experienced, but I guarantee you, not better trained. So to get our fighters ready, I've organized a scrimmage of sorts. We'll take on fighters at the MMA Academy next week, and then the week after, they'll enter in our cage."

"Who fights first?" Nong asks.

"Next week, you and Hector. Then Meghan and Jackson, the week after."

"Great!" Nong says and looks for high fives.

"You'll see what it's like to fight people who don't know your strengths or your weaknesses, nor do you know anything about them. Well, with one exception."

"What do you mean?" Jackson asks.

Mr. Hodge tells Hector that he'll be fighting a kid named Eddie Garcia who used to train at the dojo, but he left. Hector told Jackson once it was because of a personal issue between the two of them, but Jackson thinks it's because Eddie could never beat Jackson as top heavyweight. *If Eddie's fighting Hector, then that means somebody else will be fighting heavyweight*, Jackson reasons. It will be his first real test as a fighter.

⬛ ⬛ ⬛ ⬛ ⬛ ⬛

"So, you ready?" Tyresha asks Jackson. They're both working the speed bag.

"You're not," Jackson says, watching her speedy but unfocused movements. "Look, this is how you work with the bag."

Jackson shows Tyresha the right way to work the bag, just like Mr. Hodge taught him. "Striking is about speed but also precision."

"And power. Man, you crushed that poor kid Rex," Tyresha says. She stops punching.

"Hey, what are you stopping for?" Jackson says, exaggerating a fake-serious look. "You have to work every second if you want power like this." His smile breaks through as he flexes.

"Doesn't all work and no play make you boring?" Tyresha asks.

Jackson, done teasing, punches the bag harder, faster, and meaner. "No, it'll make me a champion."

Tyresha shakes her head and then puts her hands on her hips. "Jackson, I've been a champion. It feels great for about a week, and then it goes away. Then you're just you again."

Jackson throws an overhand left that smacks the bag. He mirrors Tyresha with his hands on his hips as the bag keeps vibrating, bouncing back and forth like the feeling in his gut.

"You can't let what you do define who you are," she says. "Know what I'm saying?"

Jackson doesn't answer. Though the bag has been hit a thousand times, there's still a little shine on it. Jackson sees his face in the reflection.

"So who are you, Jackson James?" Tyresha asks.

"What do you mean?" Jackson stares at his face, distorted in the vinyl.

"If someone asks who is Tyresha Harris, I tell 'em that she's the icy girl who'll lay the smackdown on your sorry self if you get in her face."

Jackson laughs at her swagger. He goes back to throwing hard punches without answering the question.

CHAPTER 7

"So Joseph and I can't attend this spar Mr. Hodge set up?" Jackson's mom asks over Saturday breakfast. Joseph is in his room, claiming sickness, but Jackson guesses he's hungover.

"No, Mr. Hodge doesn't allow friends or family. You know that."

"Maybe he'd make an exception. Didn't you say that you'd be fighting at the other dojo? Do you want me to talk to him?" Jackson's mom is relentless. "Jackson, I'd like to see you fight."

Jackson laughs.

"What's so funny?"

"Just how most moms don't say that to their sons," Jackson replies.

"You're not most sons," his mom says. "I know MMA wasn't my first choice. But after your dad died . . ." she trails off. "Seeing you so angry? Following the wrong people?" She exhales. "You needed an outlet."

Jackson gives a silent nod.

"But you've built so much confidence. You've really focused yourself. Jackson, your father would be so very, very proud of you."

Jackson hopes his mom doesn't notice the goose bumps rise on his arm, but he can't bring himself to agree with her. The truth, he thinks, is that his father would be ashamed of his son associating with someone like Hakeem. The last conversation they had before his dad went overseas for the last time was about Jackson making good choices. But after his dad's death, hanging with Hakeem seemed to be the answer. Life was hard his freshman year, but Hakeem made everything easy, just like he's making it easy for Joseph now. Jackson knows how easy it can be to lose yourself in the crowd and follow orders.

"I hope to make him proud next week," Jackson says. "I'll ask Mr. Hodge about letting you watch."

"On second thought, don't. I understand that he has his rules," his mom says and smiles. "You make one exception to your rules, and before you know it, you lose control of everything."

⊏ ⊏ ⊏ ⊏ ⊏ ⊏

"Take him down, Jackson!" Mr. Matsuda yells as Jackson battles Marcus Robinson, the top fighter in the dojo. With the scrimmage spar coming up, Mr. Hodge and Mr. Matsuda have kicked up Jackson's and Meghan's training. Although Marcus is just a flyweight, Jackson's having a hard time taking him down. Jackson tries single-leg and double-leg takedowns, but Marcus sprawls. Jackson's attempt at a sweeping hip throw results in Marcus stuffing him into the mat.

"Take him down, Jackson!" Mr. Matsuda repeats.

Banging his gloves together, Jackson rushes

toward Marcus and starts throwing kicks. Marcus responds in kind. When Jackson sees Marcus's left leg land awkwardly after a blocked kick, he takes Marcus down with a hip throw and mounts him on the mat.

Mr. Matsuda blows his whistle and rushes into the cage. "What was that, Jackson?"

Jackson is stunned. Why is Mr. Matsuda angry? Jackson did what he'd said. "A takedown."

"When you use that hip throw, you've got to sweep your leg out. That will knock his leg out from under him," Mr. Matsuda explains. "Marcus, you're excused. Jackson, stay here."

"Yes, sir."

"Pick one of the new fish to help you with this drill."

Jackson doesn't even fake taking time to think. "Tyresha."

"Tyresha, new fish, get in here," Mr. Matsuda says. "Let him take you down."

Tyresha does as she's told. This time Jackson executes the sweeping hip throw perfectly. She crashes hard to the mat in a way that not only gets Jackson position but would impress judges. He wants to ask her if she's all right, but Mr. Matsuda's staring at them both.

"Again!"

"Yes, sir!" They get up, and again, Jackson executes the move. But Mr. Matsuda keeps making Jackson repeat it over and over. Ten times, Tyresha crashes to the mat.

"When's my turn?" Tyresha finally asks and then laughs.

Mr. Matsuda scowls. "Not until I say it is, new fish," he answers. "Do ten more, Jackson."

Another ten times, Jackson takes Tyresha down with a perfect sweeping hip throw, but on the last time, Mr. Matsuda doesn't blow the whistle. "Submit her, Jackson, do it now!"

Tyresha reacts quicker than Jackson and gets closed guard, hooking her feet behind Jackson's legs. Jackson tries to grab an arm, but for a new fighter, Tyresha's learned fast to get guard. She keeps moving, making Jackson work. Jackson powers up, breaks guard, and stands.

Tyresha stands and they return to their fighting stance. "What was that?" Mr. Matsuda asks.

"I couldn't get position," Jackson explains.

"You don't get position, Jackson; you take it!"

Jackson hangs his head. "Yes, sir."

"Now, Tyresha, it's your turn. I want to see ten perfect sweeping hip throws." Like a tackling dummy in football, Jackson takes the punishment. After the last throw, Mr. Matsuda doesn't blow the whistle and lets them continue. "I want to see someone tap. No striking."

Before Tyresha can control him, Jackson pops his hips and escapes. But rather than going to his feet, he gets side control again. Tyresha's tilted away from him when Jackson gives a final thrust with his knees to get under her on his back. Tyresha tucks her chin, but Jackson bullies his hands underneath her defense. "Sorry," he whispers and he gets the hold.

"Right arm top!" Mr. Matsuda yells, and Jackson complies until he has the rear naked choke locked in tight. Mr. Matsuda blows the whistle. "Now, let me show you how to escape."

Mr. Matsuda motions for Tyresha to get up, and he takes her place. "Go ahead!"

Jackson takes up where he left off and wraps the choke on Mr. Matsuda, but the skilled teacher almost immediately drives his right arm under Jackson's to create distance and relieve the pressure. Jackson keeps trying to work back the choke, but Mr. Matsuda's not letting him lock it in. He's fighting with his feet, not allowing Jackson to lock his legs. Jackson knows he can't submit Mr. Matsuda this way, so he starts to move back into side control. When he takes his left arm off Mr. Matsuda's neck, in an instant, Mr. Matsuda grabs the arm, pops out from the hold, and locks Jackson's arm in a Kimura. Jackson taps.

"How did you do that?" Jackson asks.

"You make one mistake and it's over," he says. "There are no second chances in the cage."

"Well done, Jackson," Mr. Hodge says, approaching. "Takedowns are not about strength. They're about leverage and balance. You forget that sometimes because you're so powerful. Good job."

"You've proven you can take a new fish down," Mr. Matsuda says, putting a hand on

Jackson's shoulder, "so let's see how you can do with others." He and Mr. Hodge smile, and Jackson hears laughter behind him. He turns around. Standing outside of the ring in single file is every student, male and female, in the dojo. They're in order by size, from the biggest to the smallest. Marcus is at the back of the line waiting for another shot. "Let's go!" Mr. Matsuda slaps Jackson's back.

Jackson smacks his gloves together as he looks over the mob waiting for him. He's got the firepower, but they've got the odds. Kind of like his dad the day he died in Afghanistan.

CHAPTER 8

"Jackson, I need you to make dinner tonight," Jackson's mom says when she calls him after school. "I have to work late."

Jackson sighs. She works late a lot—but then again, so does he. Despite having a lot of schoolwork, Jackson is going to the dojo on weeknights for the teen workouts and weekends with the adults to get ready for his fight. And, he admits to himself, to see Tyresha.

"Is Joseph home from school yet?" Jackson's mom asks.

Jackson pauses. Joseph's nowhere to be seen,

but does he tell his mom that?

"Jackson?" Jackson moves the phone away from his ear.

Jackson thinks how Joseph is probably headed for trouble with Hakeem and should be stopped. But he still can't break it to his mom.

His mom sighs. "I told him to be home after school or else."

"He called and said he was going to the library to study," Jackson lies.

"About time he did that," his mom says. "You should get some studying done yourself."

Another pause. Jackson has never lied to his mom about having Tyresha tutor him, but he's also never told her about it. Maybe she hasn't asked because she doesn't want to know.

"If you don't pull up your grades, then the Special Forces won't take you."

"I know," Jackson says. He glares at his math textbook like it's his opponent.

"I should be home around 8:30. Will you still be there?"

In his mind, Jackson's dialing Tyresha's number. "I'll be at the dojo or studying with friends." It's not a lie—he knows that a friend is all Tyresha can be, according to the rules.

⌐ ⌐ ⌐ ⌐ ⌐ ⌐

On his way to Tyresha's, Jackson takes a detour into hostile enemy territory.

"Is Hakeem home?" Jackson asks when Hakeem's mom answers the door.

"Maybe," she answers and then pulls in a drag from her cigarette. Jackson is clouded in secondhand smoke. "Hakeem! Hakeem!"

Jackson stands awkwardly on the porch waiting, feeling vulnerable.

"If he ain't here, he's probably down at the park. Why do you care, snitch?" Hakeem's mom shakes her head dismissively as she shuts the door in Jackson's face. He takes the insult like a punch and shakes it off.

Jackson pulls his hoodie tight around him. His mom must have washed his army jacket, because it was nowhere to be found this morning.

Sure enough, he sees Hakeem, Deshon, and Joseph sitting around a table at Northside Park. There's a brown paper bag in the center of the table and piles of candy, chips, and smokes. They're like pirates who cracked open a convenience store treasure chest.

"What do you want, Jackson?" Hakeem snaps as Jackson moves to the table.

"Yeah, what do you want?" Joseph parrots.

Jackson breathes deeply and exhales the cold Missouri air out his nostrils like a dragon. He glares at Hakeem fiercely. "I want you to leave my little brother alone."

"Don't be telling me what to do," Hakeem says. Joseph looks entertained.

"And you, Joseph, I want you to stop hanging around with Hakeem, or else."

"Or else what?" Hakeem doesn't raise his hands to fight. Instead, Hakeem opens his hoodie so that Jackson can see the butt of the gun in the waistband. "See, not so tough after all."

Jackson takes a step back and shakes his head. "Why don't you fight me like a man?"

Hakeem answers with a smirk on his face. "You ain't no man. You're just a rat." Joseph and Deshon laugh. Jackson stares harder and colder.

He turns to his brother.

"Hey, Joseph, I covered for you with Mom. I told her you were studying."

"I am!" Joseph bumps fists with Hakeem and then takes a swig from the bottle in the bag.

"Well, I want something from you in return," Jackson says.

"What?"

Jackson grabs the sleeve of the army coat Joseph is now wearing, pulls him up, and drops him back down on the bench before walking away. "I want my jacket back."

⬚ ⬚ ⬚ ⬚ ⬚ ⬚

"You're late," Tyresha says as they meet on the library steps.

"Sorry," Jackson says.

"What's wrong?"

Jackson doesn't answer, just turns and walks into the library.

"Jackson, come on, talk to me." Tyresha follows behind and places her hand on his shoulder, giving him goose bumps.

"Do you really want to know?"

She nods, but they don't sit. They keep moving.

"It's about my brother," Jackson starts. Quietly, he tells Tyresha everything. She listens, nods and, every now and then, touches Jackson's hand. He pours out his fears about his brother getting into serious trouble. Not just what that would mean for Joseph but also how it would hurt his mom. More than that, what it would mean to the memory of his father. His dad had died protecting people he didn't even know. "What am I willing to risk to protect my own flesh and blood from making bad mistakes? This is all so hard—you know what I'm saying?"

"Well, there's an answer for that, Jackson," Tyresha whispers. "You need something soft."

"Like what?" He turns to face Tyresha, who pulls him in and kisses him.

CHAPTER 9

"Jackson James from Missouri MMA vs. Andrew Brown from MMA Academy! You're up!" The guy running the show shouts at Jackson and Mr. Hodge.

Jackson grunts acknowledgment of the announcement as he keeps smacking the pads that Marcus is wearing. Jackson is still angry that he wasn't able to take Marcus down, a fighter weighing less than a hundred pounds. He got everybody to the ground in the gauntlet except Marcus. But he's angrier at himself for breaking the dojo rule with Tyresha. Will she be watching him fight? Will she be cheering for him? Or will she still be angry that after their kiss, Jackson gently pushed her away?

"Remember the plan?" Mr. Hodge asks. Jackson nods. "Once you get him to the ground, you can control him. Look for your shot, take it, and then take him out. Okay?"

Another nod, another grunt. Jackson bangs his gloves together. He's ready.

Mr. Hodge and Marcus go to the ring with Jackson. Mr. Matsudo stays off to the side to warm up Meghan. Hector and others sit in chairs in the dojo, and Tyresha stands in back.

Jackson stares across the ring at his opponent. Like Jackson, Andrew Brown is tall, muscled, and black. At the weigh-in, Brown smirked at him. Jackson scowled back like a master. In Brown's sarcastic expression, Jackson saw Hakeem's face taunting him.

The ref gives instructions, but Jackson is barely listening. "You'll be fighting three two-minute rounds. If there is no clear winner, I will act as the judge to decide one. Obey my instructions at all times. Protect yourself and have a good fight. Let's make this happen."

The fighters circle in the center of the ring, looking for a chance. Jackson strikes first with a low kick and a left hook, but Brown rushes forward and tees off with a flurry. Jackson's stunned but tries not to show it. Brown lands a straight right, then a left hook. He's got Jackson's heavy hands and Hector's speed—a powerful combination. Jackson fakes a takedown and then lands a solid left, but Brown answers with another right. When Jackson plants his foot to try the hip throw, Brown kicks it hard. Both his legs are hurting now. Jackson keeps moving, but most of his punches don't connect and Brown has stopped every takedown. As the whistle blows, Jackson bangs his gloves together hard. He knows he's lost the round.

"Watch his right and those kicks," Mr. Hodge says as Jackson retreats to the corner. "Sweep the leg, sweep it, okay?"

Jackson nods. For the full thirty seconds of the round break, Mr. Hodge reminds Jackson of what he needs to do to win. Sweat drips from his forehead, but he's not breathing hard. He's ready to rumble.

Jackson runs toward the center of the ring when the next whistle blows. Before Brown can strike, Jackson throws wild punches. Most don't connect, but Brown can't punch back when he's defending. On the offensive, Jackson throws two hard kicks to Brown's body. Brown tries a kick of his own, and Jackson goes for the sweep. Brown defends but leaves himself open. Jackson crushes Brown just over the left eye. *If Brown didn't have on a helmet*, Jackson thinks, *he wouldn't have a head.* Brown staggers but stays on his feet and throws a high knee.

"Take him down, Jackson, take him down!" Mr. Hodge yells, but Jackson's not listening to anything outside the ring. His senses kick into overdrive at the sight of the smirk on Brown's now bloody face.

Jackson presses the action with rights and lefts. After another leg kick, Brown starts firing back. Like some out-of-control machine, the two exchange a flurry of punches and kicks, their arms and legs flying wildly. Brown tags

Jackson twice with leg kicks and takes him down.

"Ten seconds!"

Before Brown can get a mount, Jackson is back on his feet. He's throwing hands when the whistle blows. In the corner between rounds, Mr. Hodge shouts instructions. "You're fighting his fight. He's controlling the action. You need to take him down and work a submission, understand?"

Jackson's face tells that he does: his eyes stare across the ring in steely determination, while his mouth sets in a scowl. He stands still waiting for the ref to start the round, but inside he's pacing like a caged tiger.

The fighters touch gloves and assume the fighting stance. Brown again pushes the action, side-stepping a hard right and getting a double leg. Even as he's falling to the mat, Jackson keeps throwing punches. One lands squarely on Brown's temple, and he releases Jackson before gaining control. Back on his feet, Jackson starts headhunting. No kicks, no body shots. Nothing but right hands aimed at Brown's smirking face.

Brown fakes a single leg, then hits a hard spinning backfist that knocks Jackson backward. As Jackson reaches to clinch and close the distance, Brown uses Jackson's forward momentum to slam him to the mat.

"Ten seconds!"

On the mat, Brown tries to mount Jackson, but Jackson sweeps from underneath and catches Brown in side control. Jackson pushes hard with his knees to turn Brown over, but Brown's fighting it off. A quick hammer fist splats Brown's nose as the whistle stops the fight.

The fighters touch gloves. "Good fight," Brown says.

Jackson nods. "Nice spinning backfist." He stands next to Brown, head down.

Mr. Hodge checks to see if Jackson's hurt, but Jackson shakes him off. His face is fine; his confidence is destroyed. He doesn't need to wait for the decision. He knows he lost the fight.

After the announcement, which gives two of the three rounds to Brown, and after another exchange of respect, the fighters head into the locker rooms. Jackson starts to sit down on a bench, but Mr. Hodge, who followed him in, makes him stand up. "Jackson, what is wrong with you?"

Jackson spits out his mouthpiece. "I'm sorry, I lost." Mr. Hodge crosses his arms.

"That's right. He didn't win, you lost. You decided to slug it out when you should have taken it to the ground like I told you. You looked like the untrained kid who walked into my dojo two years ago, not the athlete I know you are. You fought angry, not aggressive."

"I don't know what to say."

"You don't have to say anything. Just learn from your mistakes. Can you do that?"

Jackson gazes into the filthy locker room mirror and asks himself the very same thing.

CHAPTER 10

"These are for you." Jackson hands two tickets to Corporal Richards. "Do you think you could give one to Corporal Davis? I'd like him to see my first amateur fight."

"Might be tough, Jackson. He's in country."

Jackson shakes his head at that odd army phrase. *In country* means "out of this country." *In country* often ends with in coffin. Everything in the army seems backward, but Jackson still looks forward to joining, doing his part, and making his family proud.

"Well, I want you to see me fight."

"You know being in Special Forces is more than being tough and in good condition. You have to learn to take orders. Can you do that?" Corporal Richards says.

"Yes, sir!"

"Okay, then tell me about this arrest that got you kicked off your football team."

Jackson shifts in the hard chair. It reminds him, strangely, of the hard chairs at the St. Louis Juvenile Detention Center. "Like I said, I was running with the wrong crowd."

"Details, Jackson, details."

Jackson recounts his past: hanging with Hakeem, mobbing stores, and stealing liquor. He doesn't mention dishonoring his father's memory. He remembers it like it was yesterday: his mother confronting him, calling him a coward and follower when his father had been a hero and a leader.

Jackson's learned at the dojo how to read body language to guess a foe's next move, but he can't read Corporal Richards's face.

"So what did you learn from this experience?" Richards asks in almost a sing-song voice.

"That the food at JDC sucks, and that I should stay away from Hakeem."

"He sounds like trouble, am I right?"

Jackson puts his hand in his pocket to cover his phone with two recent texts from Hakeem. He keeps telling him not to text. Now Hakeem's taunting him.

"You need to learn to stand up for yourself and not follow the wrong people," Richards advises.

"You come to my fight, and you'll see I stand up plenty. Stand up and knock 'em down."

Corporal Richards laughs. "I'll say this— you don't lack confidence. That's a good sign."

Jackson shrugs. He doesn't want to disagree. He needs to stay on Richards's good side.

"Who are you fighting?"

"I don't know yet. My application gets approved today, since it's my eighteenth birthday."

Richards looks at his computer. "That's right. So are you ready to sign up now?"

"I still want to fight for a while, like I told you," Jackson explains. "I put so much time and effort into MMA. I did it for the training, but I guess I found I liked it."

"The love of combat is part of the warrior ethic."

Jackson looks at the American flag in the corner. It's the same size as the one handed to him at his dad's funeral. It's on the wall in his room, over the dresser filled with the photos of his dad. Jackson stares at the flag. "It's not just combat I like. It's the pride that goes with winning."

☐ ☐ ☐ ☐ ☐ ☐

"Happy birthday, son," Jackson's mom says as she hands him an envelope. She's taken him and Joseph out to a fancy restaurant. Jackson convinced himself that the big steak he devoured was good muscle fuel. His opponent may be older, but he won't be stronger. Or hungrier to win.

"Thanks, Mom," Jackson takes the envelope. He's distracted by Joseph, who is texting under the table, unbeknownst to his mother. Jackson opens the envelope, and inside the birthday card is a blank check. "What's this?"

"It's good for another year of training at the dojo if you decide to do that," Jackson's mom says with a smile. "Or good for a trip back home from basic if you join Special Forces. It depends on what you decide to do. Do you know yet?"

"Thanks, Mom," Jackson answers without really answering. It's times like this that Jackson wishes he could obey orders like at the dojo. Sweep the leg. Throw a jab. Close guard. You don't decide at the dojo, you just do.

"Bro, I got you something," Joseph says. He also hands Jackson an envelope. Jackson hides his disappointment. What he really wants is his army jacket back. Jackson could just take it from him, but he wants to test his brother: will he do the right thing and give the jacket back?

Jackson opens the envelope and inside is a wad of cash.

"Son, where did you get that?" Jackson's mom asks.

Joseph fixes Jackson with a hard stare

as if he's daring him to snitch. "I won it," Joseph answers. Jackson doesn't blink. Joseph probably stole it or sold stuff he stole to get the money.

"Won it? Doing what?" Jackson's mom asks. "I won't have you—,"

"I know a guy who placed a bet for me on a fight, no big deal." Maybe his mom can't hear the lying tremor in Joseph's voice, but Jackson does. Jackson's mom shakes her head. If she knew where he got the money from, she'd be heartbroken rather than just disappointed.

"I don't want you to do that ever again, you hear me, son?"

"I won't do it again." Joseph nods in agreement.

"Good. Now, how about some dessert?" Jackson's mom waves the waitress over to their table. While his mother talks to her, Jackson wants to finish the conversation with Joseph.

"So what fight did you bet on?" Jackson asks softly, just trying to see if Joseph tips his hand.

Joseph lifts his head up and smirks like Hakeem. "Yours. I bet you'd lose. Thanks, bro."

Under the table, Jackson pounds his hands together until his knuckles bleed.

CHAPTER 11

"Side control! Side control!" Mr. Matsuda shouts at Jackson. Jackson slips his sparring partner's guard, reverses, and gets position. His sparring partner in the Saturday adult class, Teddy Melton, is five years older. But Jackson's more experienced.

Melton's trying to fight out while Jackson keeps control, just waiting for a mistake. It doesn't take long, as Melton tries a roll through but gives up his back. He tries fighting off the choke, but Jackson gets it in deep. Mr. Matsuda blows the whistle.

"Now that's the fight you need to fight," Mr. Matsuda says as Jackson and Melton touch gloves. "Use your strength to get your opponent to ground, then control him until he tries to escape. When he tries, he'll leave an opening. Take his mistake and use it against him. Understand?"

Jackson nods his head, and sweat flies off his chin.

"Then, even if you don't submit it, you'll make him think about it," Mr. Matsuda explains. "He'll think the only way to win is a knockout, so he'll start punching. And then what?"

Jackson kisses his right fist. "Lights out!"

"Okay, let's get you in the cage with Marcus one last time before your fight next week," Mr. Matsuda says as he pats Jackson on the back. "Hey, happy birthday."

Jackson doesn't react. He climbs into the cage and waits. Mr. Hodge signals for the other fighters to stop their drills and watch the fight. Since it's a Saturday, neither Hector nor Nong is in attendance, but Meghan and Tyresha stand outside the cage. Jackson knows that the cage and Mr. Hodge's rules are the only things standing between him and Tyresha. But now that he's eighteen, he wonders if those rules still apply.

Mr. Hodge steps inside the cage and gives his normal speech about "protecting yourself." Marcus and Jackson touch gloves. They charge at each other when the whistle blows.

Marcus circles, jabs, and then circles some more. Jackson feels dizzy as Marcus keeps moving around. Jackson tries to shoot, but Marcus is too fast. He slips it or sprawls. Jackson knows that with his weight advantage, he can win if the fight goes to the ground, so he waits.

Marcus must know it too, since he doesn't even try a takedown. Kick, punch, kick. Jackson takes them all as the whistle signals the end of the first round. Between rounds, Tyresha approaches him at the side of the cage. She whispers, "Why don't you just charge him, clinch him, and submit him?"

Jackson takes out his mouthpiece. "Easier said than done. You wanna try?"

"You won't try; you'll do it!" she says matter-of-factly. "Jackson James is a fighting machine, so do it!" Jackson takes a deep breath as she walks away, her pep talk pulling him up a little taller.

The fighters touch gloves, and the whistle blows for the next round. But rather than taking a step back, Jackson charges and locks Marcus in a clinch. Marcus throws knees to the body in rapid fire. Each one connects to Jackson's ribs. As another knee smashes into his side, Jackson reaches down, grabs Marcus's leg, and they crash down together on the mat. Jackson uses his size to mount, but Marcus gets a full guard, and there's little Jackson can do. When he reaches in to snatch Marcus's arm for an Americana, Marcus is too fast and pulls Jackson's left arm toward him. He pulls guard, wraps Jackson's arm between his legs, and rolls. Jackson taps out of the armbar.

As they touch gloves after the spar, Jackson feels a wave of pain shoot through his arm and his side. Nothing's broken, but everything's bruised—most of all, his ego.

□ □ □ □ □ □

"That was some great fighting advice," Jackson says, cocking an eyebrow at Tyresha. They're in her car in the parking lot of an old video store. They can't be seen together outside the dojo, or word might get to Mr. Hodge.

"It seemed good in theory, but why would you listen to me?" Tyresha says and laughs. "You've been doing this for over two years, and I've been doing it for a few months."

"I guess I'm used to taking people's advice," Jackson says with a shrug.

"You gotta learn to trust yourself," Tyresha says with a smile.

"I guess," Jackson mumbles and then shifts in the passenger seat. He lets out a pained cry.

"You okay? Maybe you need me to kiss it and make it better?"

Jackson blushes. "That one knee really landed. I think I bruised a rib."

"Well, if you won't let me kiss you, then I

know this will make it better," Tyresha says as she opens up her purse. She pulls out a small bag of weed. Jackson grabs the bag from her.

"No, I'm not doing this. It could get me kicked out of the dojo."

Tyresha laughs before she kisses Jackson hard on the lips. "And so could this."

Again, Jackson pushes her away. "I told you, Tyresha, we can't be doing this."

Tyresha looks down, breathes, and searches for words. "Jackson, look I don't want to get you in trouble. I'm sorry."

"Trouble seems to follow me," Jackson says, then laughs.

"Maybe it's more that you follow trouble, like hanging around with people like me." Tyresha puts the bag back into her purse. "But am I really that bad of a kisser?"

"You kiss just fine. It's just that it's against the rules."

"Are you afraid of Mr. Hodge?"

"No," Jackson answers, "I'm afraid of myself. I just got to keep things under control, and the way to do that is obeying the rules."

"Rules were made to be broken," Tyresha whispers. "Besides, I won't tell anybody. Who is going to know?"

Jackson shakes his head and bangs his strong right hand against his chest. "Me."

CHAPTER 12

Jackson walks into the dojo ready to fight. He throws his coat on the floor—a coat from Goodwill, since Joseph still won't give up Jackson's army jacket—then grabs some head-gear and heads straight for his longtime dojo mates.

"Hey, look who's here!" Hector says.

Jackson responds with fist bumps for Hector and Nong. "Need all the ring time I can get."

"I heard about your fight with Marcus. Tough loss," Nong says.

Jackson starts throwing kicks against the punching bag. "Nong, didn't you tell us that defeat brews the bitter tea of victory?" He looks around for Tyresha, but she's not there. Another hard kick. "I'm countin' on it paying off in my fight this weekend."

"My money's on you," Hector says. "Not that I have any, but if I did."

"Do people really bet on amateur fights?" Jackson asks. He knows that story Joseph told was a lie to get under his skin, but he wonders. Maybe he could take that money Joseph gave him for his birthday and bet on himself. Except he's not confident he will win.

"People bet on everything," Meghan shouts. Jackson turns around and is shocked to see Meghan with a black eye. His tips for Tyresha must be paying off. Their trade has certainly worked to his advantage too, since he's doing better in math thanks to her help. If only she'd quit the dojo, he keeps thinking, then they could get together. But he can't ask her to do that. Jackson knows he's got some hard decisions to make—about Tyresha, about joining up, and about Joseph—but for now, he's gotta focus on his first fight. For his opponent, it's going to be just another fight. But for Jackson, it's a launching pad.

Jackson joins Hector in various drills. His rib still hurts, but he fights through it. He'd like to spar again with Marcus to get his win back but doesn't want to risk injury.

"Jackson, in the cage," Mr. Hodge shouts. Jackson obeys and jogs to the cage. "Everybody"—the room gets quiet fast as people turn toward Mr. Hodge— "as you know, Jackson has his first amateur fight on Saturday. I expect all of you to be there to support him. But the best thing you can do tonight is give him a good, hard spar. Who's first?"

"I am!" A loud voice comes from the back of the room. Jackson doesn't recognize the voice until he sees Rex step forward. It's the first time he's seen him since Rex's first night in the gym, the night that Jackson concussed him with a hard right.

"Three rounds, one minute each, full contact MMA," Mr. Hodge shouts. Rex smiles before putting in his mouth guard.

After the whistle blows and they touch

gloves, Jackson starts circling. Rex is short but compact. Jackson has the reach, size, and experience, but he can't land anything. Rex is almost turtling from the stand-up, taking shots he deflects, but not offering any offense.

"Fight with aggression, Rex, not anger!" Mr. Matsuda shouts. "Fight, Rex, fight!"

Rex responds and throws quick jabs. Jackson blocks most of them, but one gets through. It's a solid shot, but Jackson barrels ahead for the clinch. Another jab connects before Jackson grabs him. Knees, elbows, and punches trade back and forth as the round ends.

The second round begins with more of the same. Rex won't make a mistake because he's barely making any moves. He's waiting for Jackson to slip up, and Jackson knows it.

Jackson throws a right, then a kick. The kick leaves his chin open, and Rex reaches with a wild left hook that leaves him off-balance. Just like he'd practiced a thousand times, Jackson seizes the moment. He grabs Rex's leg and then sweeps the foot. Rex hits the mat with a thud after Jackson's perfect sweeping hip throw. On the mat, Jackson doesn't mount but gets side control. Rex is frantically trying to get up. Jackson eases off, allowing Rex to roll to his stomach. Before Rex knows what's happened, Jackson's got the rear naked choke, and Mr. Hodge stops the match.

Jackson helps Rex up and then takes out his own mouth guard. "Great fight."

Rex shakes his head in disgust as he removes his guard. "I wanted to knock you out."

"I knew that," Jackson says as he taps Rex's gloves. "That's probably why I won. Listen to your coaches. Be aggressive but not angry."

"Hey, Jackson, how'd you get so smart?" Mr. Hodge asks with a sly smile.

"The hard way," Jackson replies.

⬚ ⬚ ⬚ ⬚ ⬚

After dressing, Jackson checks his phone. The texts from Hakeem have stopped, but he knows Joseph is still involved. Nothing has worked when he's talked to Joseph at home—not reason, shame, or threats.

Jackson thinks about calling home but

realizes since it's Wednesday, his mom's at church for another hour. He calls Tyresha.

"Where are you tonight?"

Tyresha doesn't answer.

"I saw Meghan's face. Was that you?" Jackson asks.

"So she's got a black eye?" Tyresha says. "Just like her to be better than me."

"Better than you?"

"Yeah, I gave her one black eye, but she gave me two."

"Maybe we better work on your defense," Jackson says.

Tyresha laughs. "You're pretty good at defense. You keep fighting me off, for sure."

"Look, it's not that I don't like you, it's just that I respect Mr. Hodge too much and—,"

"Jackson, I've watched you with Mr. Hodge. It's not about respect. You're afraid you're going to disappoint him. Am I right, or am I right?"

Jackson grunts. He looks at a photo of his dad and remembers feeling that same fear.

"I know you want to be a good soldier,

but great soldiers are leaders, right?" she says. "Think for yourself and about yourself for once. Ask yourself, what does Jackson James want?"

Jackson takes a deep breath. "You."

CHAPTER 13

"Congratulations, Mr. James, that's another A." Mr. Heed, Jackson's math teacher, puts Jackson's final exam down on his desk. "I don't know what you did differently this semester, but—,"

Jackson laughs so hard that everyone in the class looks at him.

"Something funny?" Mr. Heed asks.

Jackson shakes his head and stares at the test. "Nothing, sir," Jackson answers, praying he's not blushing. He's not sure if it's good or bad to find out the day before his fight that all his studying with Tyresha really paid off.

"So, I understand you're celebrating graduating from high school by fighting?" Mr. Heed asks.

Jackson doesn't like to talk about his MMA career at school. Usually, it only brings trouble. He starts giving just the basics about his fight tomorrow night, but he doesn't get far before Mr. Heed's classroom phone rings. "Yes," Mr. Heed answers and then looks at Jackson. "He's right here."

When Mr. Heed hangs up, Jackson braces himself.

"Jackson, you need to go to the principal's office," Mr. Heed says. "Now." There's urgency in Mr. Heed's tone. Jackson should be celebrating his last few days of school, but instead, for the first time in years, he's getting called to the office. He can't imagine why, but in his experience, going to the office is never a good thing.

ᴄ ᴄ ᴄ ᴄ ᴄ ᴄ

"Jackson, go on inside," Principal Shepard's assistant says. She uses the same tone Mr. Heed had. There's a seriousness and a sadness in it that remind Jackson of how people spoke at his dad's funeral. He opens the door and understands why as he sees Hakeem standing in the office with handcuffs around his wrist. The police officers hold out another pair for Jackson.

"Don't say anything," Hakeem hisses at Jackson.

"What's going on?" Jackson asks Principal Shepard, who's shaking his head.

"Jackson, I'm ashamed of you," he says. "I really thought you'd learned from your past mistakes. But—,"

"I didn't do anything!" Jackson says, looking around in confusion as a cop puts on the cuffs too tight. They lead Hakeem and Jackson out toward the cruiser. Since most people are in class, they only pass by a few other students on their way out of school, but that won't matter. People will know; everybody talks.

"Don't you dare say anything," Hakeem whispers once they reach the car. The cops read them their rights and shuffle them into the backseat.

"What is going on? What did I do?" Jackson keeps asking. He's told only that he's under arrest—not what for. Looking out the police car windows, he thinks about how far he's come in the past three years. Yet he's right back in the same place with the same person.

⸺ ⸺ ⸺ ⸺ ⸺ ⸺

He's booked into the JDC and put in a holding cell while an officer contacts his mother. One of the cops walks by and Jackson yells out. "This is a mistake. What am I doing in here?"

The cop slows and finally faces Jackson. "Robbery, son, and it's no mistake." He seems pleased with himself.

"I didn't do anything. You have to listen to me!" Jackson shouts.

The cop laughs. "Son, a picture is worth a thousand words." He takes a photograph from a large envelope. It looks like a security camera photo, time-stamped from last night. When he was with Tyresha. In the photo are twenty bodies crowding a small corner store, but only two faces are visible. One is Hakeem, stuffing his hoodie full of merchandise; the other is another black male also stuffing merchandise into a jacket. An army jacket. With the initials *JJ*.

CHAPTER 14

Jackson sits in the small cell and closes his eyes to distract himself. He visualizes his fight and sees himself doing just like Mr. Matsuda tells him to do: get side control. If he pushes his opponent over, he'll get his back and choke him out. If he pulls the guy back, he'll get the mount, where he can knock him out or work for a guillotine choke or another submission.

But as Jackson waits for his mom, he considers his options. They're all bad. If he tells the truth that it's his brother in the photo, then Joseph is in trouble. If he takes the fall for his brother, then everything he's worked so hard for the past three years will be lost. Even if he serves up his brother, then he needs an alibi of where he was, which means admitting being with Tyresha. If his mom finds out, she might tell Mr. Hodge, and then they'll be in trouble.

He recalls being in the same kind of room three years ago. He had nothing: his dad was dead. Playing football, the only thing that mattered to him even a little, would be taken away. Jackson's crime then was hanging around the wrong people. His crime now is letting his brother do the same thing. *Somehow*, Jackson thinks, *that's even worse*. Waiting around the JDC seems worse now too—scarier, since he's got more to lose.

If six minutes in the MMA cage can seem like an hour, then the hour he's spent in the cell waiting for his mother seems like an eternity. When the door opens and she's standing there with tears in her eyes, Jackson can only return the emotion.

The corrections officer escorts Jackson and his mom to a small room. The C.O. leaves them to sit down in the hard chairs provided. Between them is a small table with a brown envelope lying in the middle.

"We won't need that long," Jackson's mom says. "There's been a mistake."

The C.O. makes a half-laughing, half-coughing sound as he shuts the door.

His mom reaches for the envelope, but Jackson snatches it. He holds it against his chest, pulling it tight like a choke hold.

"Jackson, what is in that envelope? What is going on?"

Jackson looks upward. What would his dad want him to do? His dad died protecting other people. Wouldn't he want Jackson to sacrifice for his brother? But if Joseph got away with it, then he'd keep making the same mistakes and hanging with the wrong people. Mr. Matsuda is wrong: side control isn't the best position. It's the hardest, because it forces you to choose. Choose wrong, and you might be the one who ends up pinned or tapping out.

"Jackson!" his mom shouts, something she never does, bringing him back to reality.

"I'm talking to you!" She looks angry but also confused and a little afraid.

"I'm sorry I let you down," Jackson mumbles. "I'm sorry I let dad down."

"No, I know there's been a mistake. I know you, Jackson. This is not who you are now."

Closing his eyes, Jackson remembers being unable to answer when Tyresha asked him, "Who are you?"

Am I good brother? he wonders. *And if so, what does that mean?*

Jackson's mom works hard to calm herself. "Jackson, let's sit and talk. Tell me what's going on, please."

Jackson says nothing, just shakes his head back and forth

"What are you thinking, Jackson? Talk to me, please! What are you doing?"

With a hard stare fixed on the table in front of him, Jackson says, "Deciding."

CHAPTER 15

"Jackson, are you ready?" Mr. Hodge asks. Jackson bangs his gloves together.

"I've been waiting for this for two years," Jackson answers.

"Me, too, Jackson," Mr. Hodge says. "Do you remember what you said that first night when I asked everyone to introduce themselves? Everybody was talking about their black belts."

Jackson laughs. "And I said the only belt I had was the one holding up my pants."

"But that's not true now," Mr. Hodge says. "You stuck with the program. You got your belts, and you're a top-notch fighter. You can win this fight tonight."

"But you need to listen to us and do exactly as we say," Mr. Matsuda chimes in. "You didn't do that in your spar with the MMA Academy kid, and you lost to a fighter you should have destroyed."

Jackson nods his head and bangs his gloves together again. He rocks back and forth on the small stool in the locker room as Mr. Matsuda goes over the game plan. Every now and then, Mr. Hodge interrupts to ask Jackson a question. His answers are brief, to the point.

"He who controls the fight, wins the fight," Mr. Matsuda says and then pats Jackson on the back. "Nobody controls your destiny but you."

Jackson wonders how true that is, since he just decided his brother's destiny for him this morning. His mom is another face in the crowd outside, his brother's in jail, and his dad's in heaven. *Nobody is where they belong*, Jackson thinks, *except me once I step into that cage.*

⬛ ⬛ ⬛ ⬛ ⬛ ⬛

"You're up after this fight," Mr. Hodge says. "I'll leave you alone."

Alone, Jackson thinks, *is the last thing I want to be.* He stops punching the air and heads for his locker. He takes out his phone and pulls up the recent numbers. Tyresha picks up. Jackson can hear the noise of the crowd around her.

"Jackson, what are you doing? You should be thinking about your fight," she says.

"I don't want to think about it. I just want it to happen," Jackson says.

"You're going to win. I know it." Tyresha says. "I'm in the second row. Look for me."

Jackson doesn't answer. With everything he's been through the past forty-eight hours, what had been the most important thing in his life doesn't seem to mean much. Perspective packs a mean punch: it doesn't knock you out; it wakes you up. Jackson hopes Joseph reaches the same conclusion.

"Are you there?" Tyresha asks.

Jackson doesn't say anything. In his silence, he hears the crowd swell like there's been a knockout or submission. His fight is next; his time is now.

"I have to go," Jackson says.

"Break his leg, JJ!"

Jackson laughs. "Which one? His right or his left?"

"You decide."

CHAPTER 16
TALE OF THE TAPE FOR FRIDAY NIGHT FIGHTS

	JACKSON JAMES	STEVE WILSON
AGE	18	33
HEIGHT	6'0"	5'10"
REACH	75"	71"
RECORD	0-0	2-4

CHAPTER 17

Jackson listens to the ref's instructions, but his stare is fixed on his opponent. For a second, Steve Wilson reminds Jackson of the cop who arrested him, but Jackson pushes his anger down. Aggression wins fights—not anger. Instinct, not emotion, must control him.

After a brief feeling-out period, Wilson rushes in, but Jackson fights him off. Pushing forward with jabs and kicks, Jackson fights off Wilson's underhook and an over/under take-down attempt. Landing a hard right, Jackson escapes from Wilson's clutches. Jackson moves to the center and pursues Wilson, pressing until he's got him near the cage again. When Wilson tries a knee, Jackson catches it, trips the foot, and pushes him to the mat with a sweeping heel throw. The crowd cheers as Jackson works some ground-and-pound from inside Wilson's guard. He looks for a submission, but Wilson's chin is tucked while he throws short punches.

"Ten seconds," the ref calls.

With no chance of submission, Jackson stands out of Wilson's guard. Wilson starts to get up, but Jackson throws a right that puts Wilson down. Jackson leaps on top, pounding the older fighter, who is breathing heavily and bleeding from the nose.

When the bell rings, Jackson heads to his corner. Part of him wants to look into the crowd for his mom and for Tyresha, but he's got to keep his head in the fight.

"Good first round," Mr. Hodge says. "Ground him, pound him, then finish him."

"He's scared of you, so use it," Mr. Matsuda adds. "You've got control. Now keep it!"

Wilson lands a sloppy left hook to start the second round. Jackson responds with a harder right. As Jackson tries to follow with a left, Wilson gets him in the clinch. Jackson changes levels, drops down, lifts Wilson around both legs, and slams him hard into the mat. As Wilson tries to get back to his feet, Jackson grabs his ankle and drives him back to the canvas. Wilson scoots on his hips, and they're pressed against the cage. Jackson drives hard with his legs, escapes the guard, and gets side control. He punishes Wilson using knees and elbows. Wilson turns and gives Jackson his back, but he tucks his head so Jackson can't get the rear naked choke. When Wilson assumes the turtle position, the ref yells at him to start fighting back.

At the ten-second call, the ref stands both of the fighters back up. Wilson shoots in, but Jackson sprawls and attempts a standing guillotine choke. Wilson escapes and the fighters exchange wild punches. Wilson lands several hard shots as the bell ends the round. The punches hurt, but not as bad as the one Jackson throws hard against his own right leg, taking out his frustration.

Mr. Matsuda looks less pleased this time. "Jackson, the end of that round was like the fight you lost, you know that? He can't beat you—only you can. Be aggressive, not angry, if you want to win!"

As Jackson bends over, sweat pours off and forms a puddle on the mat. Matsuda fires questions at Jackson as quick as kicks. Jacksons answers each with a quick nod to show he understands. His head moves back and forth rhythmically; Jackson needs to find the same rhythm and focus in the cage.

Mr. Matsuda grabs Jackson's chin and forces him to look him in the eye. "So? Are you going to finish him or not?"

Jackson's eyes blaze. When the bell rings, he bangs his gloves together, takes a deep breath to focus, and charges out of his corner. Wilson avoids an early kick and lands a looping right hook. But Jackson answers with a right, left, and a harder right. The last one leaves Wilson staggering, and he slumps against the cage. Jackson tries another right and a takedown, but Wilson gets him off-balance in the clinch. Wilson shoots, aiming for Jackson's leg. To defend, Wilson puts his head down, and that's all that Jackson needs. He sinks a guillotine choke. Wilson reaches up, trying to unlock Jackson's arms, and in doing so gives Jackson the opportunity to wrap his right leg around Wilson's back. Jackson has total control of his head and neck.

Jackson squeezes hard, knowing full well the pain and pressure Wilson's feeling in every cell of his body. With his eyes closed, teeth clinched, and his muscles taut, Jackson holds for the submission.

"That's it," the ref yells, tapping Jackson on the shoulder as Wilson taps the mat.

◻ ◻ ◻ ◻ ◻ ◻

"Forgive me if I'm not in the mood for celebrating," Jackson's mom says when he meets her at the car. "I'm proud of you. I know your father would be too."

"I fought a smart fight, but he wasn't much competition."

"That's not what I'm talking about," his mom says. Jackson looks away so he doesn't have to watch his mom cry, like when he told her what Joseph had been doing with Hakeem. Telling his mom didn't feel like snitching, especially since Joseph's decisions almost cost Jackson everything that mattered to him. The thing to do now, he thought, is convince Joseph to do the right thing—the hard thing—and turn against Hakeem.

"You really think Dad would be proud?" Jackson whispers, his expression softening.

"I know it. But that's not as important as how you feel. Do you feel proud?" Jackson's mom looks him straight in the eyes before they climb into the car.

Jackson puts his earbuds in to drown out her questions and his lack of answers.

CHAPTER 18

"Where are we going?" Joseph asks. Both Jackson and his mom are silent as they drive away from the JDC. The judge let Joseph go home pending trial or a plea deal, but Hakeem will still be detained because of repeated juvenile offenses.

"This is garbage," Joseph protests. "I didn't do nothing."

Jackson turns and points his finger at his young brother. "When this is over, I want Dad's jacket back or else." He'd let Joseph use his imagination to fill in the details.

"Mom, did you hear that?" Joseph whines.

But Jackson's mom says nothing. She just keeps driving. After a few minutes of silence, she slows and pulls over.

"What's going on?" Joseph asks.

"Get out of the car!" Jackson's mom shouts at her younger son. He obeys but stops in his tracks when he sees where they are. It's Hakeem's house.

Jackson's mother bangs on the door. It takes a while, but eventually Hakeem's mother answers. She looks down at Jackson's mother. "What do you want?"

"We need to talk about this situation," Jackson's mother says.

"Ain't nothing to talk about," Hakeem's mother says. "You raised two snitches."

"And you raised a thief!"

Hakeem's mother turns away from Jackson's mom and stares right at Jackson. "And who do you think taught him?"

Jackson's mom shakes her head in anger—or maybe it's the shame and regret that Jackson's feeling as well.

"I don't want to see your son around Joseph again. Understood?" Jackson's mom says in an unnaturally calm voice.

"Are you threatening me?"

"No, she's not," Jackson says as he takes a step closer. "She's telling you how it's going to be. Look, trust me, you don't want to make this woman mad. She's a warrior."

"Your son has been nothing but trouble to my boys," Jackson's mother continues. "He got Jackson to—,"

Hakeem's mother laughs. "My boy didn't get Jackson to do nothing. It was his idea!"

"I don't believe you!" Jackson's mom shouts.

"Maybe he can try that 'reformed hero' crap on others, but I know what your son is," Hakeem's mother says as she lights up a smoke.

"I don't care about what happened three years ago. I care about what is happening now. You can't replay the past. You bury it, or it buries you. Hakeem is to stay away from my sons."

Hakeem's mom inhales the smoke and takes in Jackson's mom's angry brown eyes.

"This is garbage," Joseph yells and walks

toward the street. "I don't need you telling me what to do or who to be friends with. I can think for myself."

Jackson shakes his head. *Obviously not*, he thinks. Like in the cage, you might think you're ready to take on anything, but it takes years of absorbing the blows to really learn how to fight. "No, Joseph you can't."

"Shut up, Jackson, I don't need to listen to you."

"You don't need to, but you will. And do you know why?" Jackson leaves his mom and Hakeem's mom standing by the door. He towers over his little brother. "Because it's the right thing to do. Believe me, deciding what's right and wrong can be the hardest thing in the world."

Joseph stares at his brother, but he's no match. In just seconds, Joseph blinks and heads back toward the car as if Jackson were leading him from two steps behind.

With one more glare at Hakeem's mom, Jackson's mom joins her sons at the car and starts the engine.

The drive back to their house is stone silent: no words, music, nothing.

Once the car stops, Joseph starts to open the door, but the locks click shut. Just like when the cage door shuts, Jackson knows a moment of truth is just seconds away.

"Now, you listen to me, the both of you," Jackson's mom says. She's got the same tone she showered all over Hakeem's mother. "Hakeem's mother was right about you, Jackson. You are a leader, and I expect you to continue to step up at home, at school and, because it matters to you, in the cage."

Like when Mr. Hodge yells instructions, Jackson answers with a firm nod of his hard head.

"And you, Joseph, we're not doing this," Jackson's mom turns to face Joseph in the backseat. Her glare is worthy of a fierce fighter at a UFC weigh-in.

Joseph shrinks in the seat. "What do you mean 'we'?" he asks.

"This family, we are not falling apart. Today it was my turn to stand up, but tomorrow it might be your turn. We've already lost one member of this family. We will not lose another."

Jackson smiles, but not where his mom can see because he knows how serious she is. He thinks how, with a hero for a father, a warrior for a mother, and a fighter like him for a brother, there's no way Hakeem or his mom wins. No way that Joseph loses himself to the street. Jackson's family is as strong as the cage.

CHAPTER 19

When Jackson walks into the dojo the Monday after his fight, Hector, Meghan, Nong, and Tyresha applaud him. Since he's eighteen, it's Jackson's last practice with the teen class. Everyone—that is, almost everyone—is happy to see him.

"I want another chance," Rex says, approaching.

"Listen, Rex, we had a second fight. You lost it," Jackson reminds him.

"That first fight was my first night. Do you really think that counts?" Rex asks. "Do you think everything you did when you were younger and stupid should be held against you?"

Jackson shakes his head in agreement. "But you've only been fighting a few months."

"I'm a quick learner."

Jackson laughs. "No, you're not."

"What do you mean?"

Jackson kisses his fist. "A quick learner would know you don't want none of this again."

Rex puts his fist out, and Jackson bumps back. "How about tomorrow after class you come by and we'll go again. I know you don't practice with us anymore, but I'm up for a spar."

"Sure thing, Rex, but I think you'll regret it," Jackson says. "And trust me, I know a lot about regrets. But hey, you can't win a fight looking backward."

"You look straight ahead until—," Rex starts, but Jackson finishes.

"The other guy blinks."

⊏ ⊏ ⊏ ⊏ ⊏ ⊏

"Mr. Hodge, can I talk with you?" Jackson asks.

Mr. Hodge nods and motions for Jackson to join him in his office. "I know what you want."

Jackson's confused. Does Mr. Hodge know he's come to talk with him about Tyresha?

"You want to know when you can fight again, right?"

Jackson breathes a sigh of relief. "I'm ready."

"You need to wait thirty days, but I'll get you signed up, if you still want to do this." Mr. Hodge motions for Jackson to sit down across from him in the small, trophy-filled office. "Weren't you headed to the army?"

Jackson shrugs instead of answering.

"Well, when you came in, you said that you were mainly interested in the training, and I've got to say, you've been a demon. You may not be the best fighter here, but you're the best-conditioned athlete."

"Marcus is tops, I agree."

Mr. Hodge shakes his head. "No, Jackson, you could be better than him. You have more tools, and I've always thought you were a natural athlete. You just have to want it more."

Jackson pauses, thinking that over. "Mr. Hodge, how can you say that after everything I put in?"

"After I spoke with your mom and she dropped you off here for the first time, I knew you had what it took. You were lost and angry, and you needed something only MMA could give."

"Bruises? Pulled muscles?" Jackson quips.

Mr. Hodge laughs and puts his hand on Jackson's shoulder. "No, self-confidence. You needed to prove something to yourself, and I think you've done it, both in the gym and the ring."

"If I'm all that, then how come you say I don't want it more?" Jackson asks with intensity.

Mr. Hodge points at Hector. "You see, for Hector—and so many of these other fighters—fighting is their life. It's all they care about. But for you, Jackson, it's always been a means."

"A means?"

"You turned eighteen, and you didn't join the army. Why not?"

Jackson bangs his gloves together. "I've

fallen in love with fighting. But joining the service was my first love. It's hard."

"That's what I mean. I've done both, Jackson, and both have their rewards. But you can't do either to the best of your ability until you decide."

"What do you think I should do?" Jackson says.

"You have to think and decide for yourself," Mr. Hodge says. "You're a warrior either way. You could be a leader either way."

Jackson laughs. "It's easier to just do what you're told. Be a good soldier."

"But that's not who you are anymore, is it?"

Jackson nods in agreement. "No."

"That's good."

Jackson looks over Mr. Hodge's shoulder at the American flag in the corner of the dojo. "My dad was a leader. He was a company commander. He was wounded on his first tour. He could've left the army on disability or could've stayed stateside, but that's not what he wanted."

"What did he want?"

"I guess he wanted a second chance. On his

first tour, there were some losses in the unit. I think he always blamed himself—that's what my mom said. So he decided to return. He went back and never came home."

Mr. Hodge starts to say something, but he stops when Jackson starts to cry. Mr. Hodge passes by Jackson and closes the door. As Jackson continues to cry, Mr. Hodge says nothing. He just puts his strong arm on Jackson's shaking shoulders.

"Thinking about my dad—it's sad, but I also get so angry."

Mr. Hodge's hand on Jackson's shoulder reminds Jackson of his dad. "Which one is stronger?"

"Neither," Jackson says as he wipes his eyes. "Mostly I'm just proud."

⬚ ⬚ ⬚ ⬚ ⬚ ⬚

Jackson finds Tyresha in the dojo. They find a corner and pretend to spar during the takedown drill. "I just got done talking to Mr. Hodge."

"Did you tell him?" Tyresha wraps her hands tightly around Jackson's neck.

"I wanted to, but then, I don't know. We got sidetracked." Jackson tells Tyresha about the conversation, trying not to get emotional in front of her. "Now might not be the best time."

"No, Jackson, we can't wait any longer. Besides, sounds like you both got your guard down. Let's do it now, together."

Jackson wraps his hands around the back of Tyresha's neck. "You think that's a good idea?"

"If there's one thing I know about Mr. Hodge, it's that he respects people showing him respect." Tyresha releases Jackson and waves over Mr. Hodge.

Jackson lets Tyresha do most of the talking, trying to read Mr. Hodge's emotions.

Hodge looks back and forth between the two. Finally, he sighs. "I'm sorry, but just like the military, it's bad to fraternize. One of you will need to—,"

"Leave? Okay, I quit." Tyresha taps Mr. Hodge's arm and looks at Jackson. "You've sacrificed enough."

"You're sure?" Mr. Hodge asks.

"Positive. I can train elsewhere."

"You can finish up today. So for now, get back to work." Mr. Hodge walks away.

"Thank you," Jackson whispers into Tyresha's ear as he prepares to finish the drill.

"You're welcome, Jackson James," she whispers, scooping Jackson's legs out from beneath him. As he crashes to the mat, Jackson can't help but laugh.

CHAPTER 20

There's a buzz in the dojo, and not just because of the rematch between Jackson and Rex. Eyebrows rise as Tyresha walks to the cage with Jackson, her left hand on his right glove.

When Rex comes to the cage, he's not wearing a shirt. Jackson can tell that he's been working out. He's not the sleek Golden Gloves striker, but he's bulked up so that he weighs maybe only a few pounds less than Jackson. *That's good*, Jackson thinks. *Then Rex won't have any excuse when he loses.*

Mr. Hodge calls the two to the center of the

ring. Because Rex is just sixteen, Mr. Hodge put the fight in the ring instead of the cage. *But it won't matter if there are four or eight sides*, Jackson thinks. *Rex has no place to run.*

Tyresha kisses Jackson on the cheek. She's dressed in street clothes, wearing his army jacket. Joseph pleaded guilty this morning, so the jacket isn't needed as evidence anymore. The prosecutor wanted Joseph to do time at the Home School, but Joseph's lawyer—a law school friend of their mom—successfully argued against it and won over the judge.

Jackson touches gloves with Rex, but it's not respectful. Even in that small display, Rex pushes Jackson, smacking his glove harder than Jackson expects. As Jackson retreats to the corner, he knows he's got the fight won. He's aggressive; Rex is angry. It's over before it begins.

Mr. Hodge blows the whistle, and Rex starts off with a flurry of punches and even a kick. They land with a lot more force than Jackson remembers Rex having, but they're not hard enough to do any damage. Rex keeps pressing while Jackson backs up, taking shots while waiting to shoot. When a big looping left misses, Jackson grabs a single leg and dumps Rex on the mat. In seconds, he's got side control and Rex is scrambling. Rex is stuck on his side, unable to generate any offense or put up any defense. Jackson works for an armbar or the Americana lock. Rex fights it off but in doing so moves his chin, allowing Jackson to slip on the rear naked choke. Jackson's got the bottom controlled but needs to get his hands up top to apply pressure. Jackson's face is buried in the back of Rex's neck, and he hears Rex struggling, fighting through the pain. The noise distracts Jackson or maybe reminds him of the pain he felt when he started MMA. The pain of feeling lost and angry.

Aggression, not anger, wins a fight, Jackson thinks, and then loosens the hold.

Rex scrambles to his feet, and the two square off again. While Rex's punches sting, they don't bite, and Jackson shakes them off. They're in the clinch when the round ends.

"You okay?" Tyresha whispers as she gives Jackson a sip of water. He nods. "You can beat him anytime, right?" Another nod. "Then why don't you?"

Jackson doesn't answer. As he waits for Mr. Hodge to blow the whistle, he stares at Rex. In Rex's face, Jackson sees pain, frustration, and doubt. Jackson sees himself when he first started MMA. He sees Joseph, feeling lost and alone, easy pickings for Hakeem. All Rex needs, Jackson knows, is to reclaim his pride.

The second round is similar: Rex strikes and Jackson answers with more strikes and takedowns. On the ground, Jackson controls Rex's every move. Rex slips out of another submission attempt and gets to his feet. Jackson follows and brings the action to him. When Rex throws a looping left, Jackson fights his instincts more than his foe. Rather than going for a takedown, Jackson throws an off-balance hook, leaving his chin wide open.

◨ ◨ ◨ ◨ ◨ ◨

"Are you okay?" Rex asks Jackson. Mr. Hodge stands between them and then raises Rex's hand.

Jackson spits out his mouth guard. "I was wrong. You were a quick learner."

Rex shrugs, smiling. "I had good teachers."

Everybody in the dojo applauds, including Tyresha once she sees Jackson quickly return to his feet. Mr. Hodge follows Jackson toward the locker room.

"What was that?" Mr. Hodge asks before they reach the door.

Jackson stops, glances at him, and shrugs. "He won."

"I think you let him win," Mr. Hodge says. "Why would you do that?"

"It seemed like the right thing to do," Jackson mumbles. "A small sacrifice."

Hodge shakes his head. Jackson knows he can't understand. It's easy to make a small sacrifice when you've already made a big one. His family made the biggest one of all.

"If you ever pull a stunt like that again, then you're gone too. Do you understand?"

Jackson nods. His jaw hurts, but his pride isn't hurt at all by allowing Rex to reclaim his.

"So why'd you do that?" Mr. Hodge asks.

Jackson pauses. He's thinking about Joseph. "Sometimes I guess you got to do the wrong thing in order to do the right thing."

Mr. Hodge looks at him, confused.

"I knew Rex needed to get his confidence and courage back," Jackson says, keeping his voice down as he takes off his gloves. "When I came in here two years ago, I didn't have those either. I was a punk, but because of you, because of this dojo, I've learned what I can be."

"And? Have you decided about the military yet?" Mr. Hodge asks.

Jackson looks at the flag in the dojo and thinks about everything it represents. But then his eyes scan the dojo itself and all the hard work, the blood, sweet, tears, and time that it's meant to him.

"Jackson?"

And just like he'd done so many times in the past, in the cage, when Mr. Hodge asked him a question, he said nothing. He just stared at the real estate below him and nodded his head.

CHAPTER 21
SIX MONTHS LATER

"Are you sure you're ready?" Sergeant Donaldson asks. Jackson turns to his mom and Tyresha. They nod, as if to remind him they support his decision.

"I've thought about this for a long time," Jackson answers. "Where do I sign?"

Donaldson hands him the paper. After he signs, Donaldson says, "Congratulations, son."

Jackson pauses like he does when anyone calls him son. If his dad were still around, would he be saying those words?

"I have something for you." Jackson reaches into his pocket. "I'm fighting again tomorrow.

It would be great if you could come, since it will be my last fight for a while."

Donaldson smiles and takes the tickets. "Well, basic isn't long," he says. "But I hope you win tomorrow night."

Jackson kisses his right fist. "Hope won't have anything to do with it."

"We can use men like you in the Army National Guard," Donaldson says. "But I thought you had your heart set on being in Special Forces, one of the elite units."

"I'm already in an elite unit at the dojo." Jackson hugs Tyresha and smiles at his mom.

"What made you decide to join the National Guard instead?"

"I want to honor my dad by joining up, but I also want to keep fighting," Jackson explains. "It's like in MMA—sometimes there's a split decision."

"I'm proud of you, son," his mother says.

Jackson nods. He's a son, brother, fighter, and soldier, but mostly he's Jackson James. And for the first time in a long time, that fact alone makes him proud.

APPENDIX
MMA TERMS

armbar: a submission achieved by locking and hyperextending the opponent's elbow

choke: any hold used by a fighter around an opponent's throat with the goal of submission. A blood choke cuts off the supply of blood to the brain, while an air choke restricts oxygen. Types of choke holds include rear naked (applied from behind), guillotine (applied from in front), and triangle (applied from the ground).

dojo: a Japanese term meaning "place of the way," once used for temples but more commonly used for gyms or schools where martial arts are taught

grappling: using wrestling and jiu-jitsu moves based on leverage and positioning, rather than striking, to control an opponent

guard: a position on the mat where the fighter on his back uses his body to guard against his opponent's offensive moves by controlling his foe's body

hammer fist: rather than hitting straight on with the knuckles, this involves striking downward using the bottom of the fist, like a hammer pounding a nail

Kimura: a judo submission hold. Its technical name is ude-garami, but it is usually referred to by the name of its inventor, Japanese judo master Masahiko Kimura.

mount: a dominant position where one fighter is on the ground and the other is on top

side control: grappling position in which a fighter is on top of his or her opponent with their bodies at a 90-degree angle

shoot: in amateur wrestling, to attempt to take an opponent down

sprawl: a strategy to avoid takedowns by shooting the legs back or moving away from a foe

submission: any hold used to end a fight when one fighter surrenders (taps out) because the hold causes pain or risk of injury

takedown: an offensive move to take an opponent to the mat. Takedowns include single leg, double leg, and underhooks.

tap: the motion a fighter uses to show he or she is surrendering. A fighter can tap either the mat or his opponent with his hand.

TKO: technical knockout. A fighter who is not knocked out but can no longer defend himself is "technically" knocked out, and the referee will stop the fight.

UFC: Ultimate Fighting Championship, the largest, most successful mixed martial arts promotion in the world since its beginning in 1993

MMA WEIGHT CLASSES

Flyweight	under 125.9 pounds
Bantamweight	126–134.9 pounds
Featherweight	135–144.9 pounds
Lightweight	145–154.9 pounds
Welterweight	155–169.9 pounds
Middleweight	170–184.9 pounds
Light Heavyweight	185–204.9 pounds
Heavyweight	204–264.9 pounds
Super Heavyweight	over 265 pounds

WELCOME TO

THE DOJO

BODY SHOT
PATRICK JONES

SIDE CONTROL
PATRICK JONES

LEARN TO FIGHT, LEARN TO LIVE, AND LEARN TO FIGHT FOR YOUR LIFE.

HEAD KICK
PATRICK JONES

TRIANGLE CHOKE
PATRICK JONES

SOUTHSIDE HIGH

ARE YOU A SURVIVOR?

The Alliance
Bad Deal
Beaten
Benito Runs
Dance Team
Deadly Drive
The Fight
Full Impact
Overexposed
Plan B
Recruited
Shattered Star

check out all the books in the

SURVIVING · SOUTH SIDE

collection